A Note to Parents

Dorling Kindersley Readers is a compelling new program for beginning readers, designed in conjunction with leading literacy experts, including Dr. Linda Gambrell, President of the National Reading Conference and past board member of the International Reading Association.

Beautiful illustrations and superb full-color photographs combine with engaging, easy-to-read stories to offer a fresh approach to each subject in the series. Each *Dorling Kindersley Reader* is guaranteed to capture a child's interest while developing his or her reading skills, general knowledge, and love of reading.

The four levels of *Dorling Kindersley Readers* are aimed at different reading abilities, enabling you to choose the books that are exactly right for your child:

Level 1 – Beginning to read
Level 2 – Beginning to read alone
Level 3 – Reading alone
Level 4 – Proficient readers

The "normal" age at which a child begins to read can be anywhere from three to eight years old, so these levels are intended only as a general guideline.

No matter which level you select, you can be sure that you are helping your child learn to read, then read to learn!

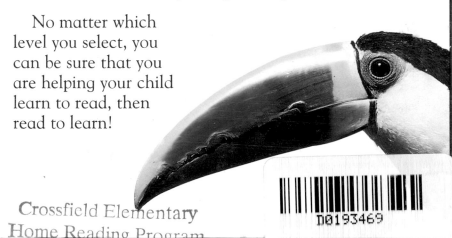

Dorling DK Kindersley

LONDON, NEW YORK, SYDNEY, DELHI, PARIS,
MUNICH and JOHANNESBURG

Project Editor Caroline Bingham
Art Editor Helen Melville
Senior Art Editor Sarah Ponder
Managing Editor Bridget Gibbs
Senior DTP Designer Bridget Roseberry
US Editor Regina Kahney
Production Melanie Dowland
Picture Researcher Frances Vargo
Jacket Designer Piers Tilbury
Illustrator Tony Morris
Indexer Lynn Bresler

Reading Consultant
Linda Gambrell, Ph.D.

First American Edition, 2000
2 4 6 8 10 9 7 5 3 1
Published in the United States by DK Publishing, Inc.
95 Madison Avenue, New York, New York 10016

Published in Great Britain by Dorling Kindersley Limited.

Library of Congress Cataloging-in-Publication Data
Gates, Phil
Horror on the Amazon: the quest for El Dorado / by Phil Gates.
p. cm. – (Dorling Kindersley readers)
Summary: Describes the conquistadores and their dangerous search for
gold, jewels, and spices in the South American jungle.
ISBN 0-7894-6639-2 (hardcover) – ISBN 0-7894-6638-4 (pbk.)
I. South America–Discovery and exploration–Spanish–Juvenile
literature. 2. Amazon River–Discovery and exploration–Spanish–Juvenile
literature. 3. South America–History–Juvenile literature. 4.
Explorers–South America–History–Juvenile literature. 5.
Explorers–Spain–History–Juvenile literature. [1. Amazon River
Region–Discovery and exploration–Spanish. 2. South America–Discovery
and exploration–Spanish. 3. Explorers.] I. Title. II. Series.

F2208.5 .G38 2000
986'.01–dc21   00-021932

Color reproduction by Colourscan, Singapore
Printed and bound in China by L Rex

The publisher would like to thank the following:
Heather Angel 7t; **Bridgeman Art Library:** Private
Colleciton 10t; **Robert Harding Picture Library:** Victor
Englebert 36t; **Hutchison Library:** Jesco von Pottkamer 16 -
17, 42 - 43; **Frank Lane Picture Agency:** Fritz Polking 29t;
Magnum Photos: Nick Nichols 12t; **Natural History
Photographic Agency:** A.N.T. 4bl; Ivan Polunin 26t; Martin
Wendler 46b; **Oxford Scientific Films:** Richard Packwood
31; **Still Pictures:** Luiz C. Marigo 5r; **Trip:** B. Masters 39

Additional photography by Geoff Brightling,
Andy Crawford, Geoff Dann, Philip Dowell,
Andreas Von Einsiedel, Dave King, Cyril Laubscher,
David Murray, Harry Taylor, Jerry Young.

see our complete
catalogue at
www.dk.com

Contents

DORLING KINDERSLEY *READERS*

READING
3
ALONE

TERROR
ON THE AMAZON

Written by Phil Gates

A Dorling Kindersley Book

A city of gold

In 1541 an army of Spanish soldiers crossed the Atlantic Ocean from Europe to South America in search of a city of gold. They hoped to become rich beyond their wildest dreams. But their dreams turned into nightmares. There was no gold and most of the soldiers died. Those who survived returned with amazing tales.

The Andes is the world's longest mountain range. It runs for 4,500 miles (7,240 km).

ANDES

•QUITO

SOUTH

The soldiers' incredible journey took them along the Amazon, one of the world's mightiest rivers. The Amazon begins in the Andes mountains of South America, then flows for 3,900 miles (6,275 km) through the steamy Amazon rainforest to the Atlantic Ocean. This rainforest is the largest on earth, and it can be a very dangerous place.

The map shows the northern part of South America.

AMAZON

MERICA

The Amazon contains more water than any other river in the world.

The Spanish soldiers were called conquistadors (kon-KEE-sta-doors), or conquerors. They were fierce, ambitious fighters who were always looking for land to conquer.

The conquistadors were a frightening force and treated people cruelly.

Cinnamon leaves

Cinnamon tree

The soldiers had heard that great riches were hidden in the rainforest. Stories told of a Land of Cinnamon, full of trees that produced fragrant spices. Many people in Europe wanted spices to flavor their food and make exotic scents. The trees in the Land of Cinnamon would be worth a fortune.

Cinnamon

Cinnamon is made by peeling thin layers of bark from cinnamon trees. These come from China and India, not, as the soldiers thought, from South America.

The conquistadors had also heard the legend of El Dorado, the Golden King. According to the stories, his body was covered with sticky gum and dusted with gold powder every morning. One day each year a boat took him to a small island in the lake beside the city of El Dorado. There he would stand as a living statue, gleaming like a piece of polished gold.

On this special day his people worshipped him by throwing sacrifices of jewels into the lake. They then feasted and danced into the night.

The conquistadors wanted to conquer the people of El Dorado and steal their gold and jewels.

The journey begins

Gonzalo Pizarro

In February 1541, the Spanish conquistador Gonzalo Pizarro set out to find the legendary cinnamon, gold, and jewels. He left the mountain town of Quito (KEE-toe) in present-day Ecuador, a country on the western coast of South America, with 210 soldiers. They were heavily armed. The soldiers always expected trouble.

The soldiers forced 4,000 terrified Indians from conquered mountain kingdoms to go with them to carry supplies and act as guides.

For food, they took 4,000 pigs. They also took 1,000 dogs, all trained to attack. After the baggage had been loaded on to llamas, the long column of people and animals set off. Their hopes were high.

Machetes are still used in South America.

Things soon began to go wrong. As the Indians hacked a path through the hot, steamy forest with machetes, they began to die. They had come from cold mountain kingdoms and could not survive the constant rain and intense heat of the rainforest.

Even worse, insects were rapidly spreading sickness. Rainforests are full of biting insects, including mosquitoes, and the men were continuously bitten.

Mosquito

Mosquitoes drink blood from people and animals by piercing the skin. They spread a deadly disease called malaria.

After struggling through the forest for five months the army built a camp and rested. Gonzalo Pizarro and 80 of his soldiers searched the land around the camp for cinnamon trees.

When they couldn't find any, they captured some Indians living in the forest and tried to force them to tell the secrets of the Land of Cinnamon.

The Indians knew there was no such place, but they were terrified. They told the conquistadors that it was a few days' march away, so they might be released and left in peace.

Chichona

The bark of the chichona tree is used to make a medicine called quinine. Quinine relieves the fever of malaria. Rainforest Indians ground the bark and made it into drinks.

The army marched deeper into the rainforest, and deeper into trouble. More of the soldiers developed sicknesses, such as malaria, which made them weak and feverish.

The Indians who lived in the Amazon knew how to use the leaves, bark, and roots of trees and plants to cure diseases. They used the chichona tree, now well-known for its medicinal uses. The soldiers didn't have this knowledge and so they suffered badly.

Strange new lands

Eight months after leaving Quito, the conquistadors reached a land of swamps and creeks and came to a river. They began to see more Indians, from tribes that had built their houses along the riverbanks.

Dugout canoe

A dugout canoe is a simple boat made by splitting a tree trunk in half and hollowing out the wood inside.

Some Indians wore flat wooden plates inside their bottom lips. Some wore feather headdresses. They looked fierce and unfriendly to the starving soldiers.

The conquistadors needed to cross the river, so they stole 18 dugout canoes from the Indians. They knew that they would have to make many journeys, back and forth, to carry themselves, their animals, and their equipment across the river. They didn't know that the horror was just about to get much worse.

Crocodile-like animals, called caymans, lazed on the mud banks beside the river. If a man or animal fell into the water, a cayman would slither in too. The soldiers could just see its eyes above the water. If the man or animal was too slow to reach the bank, the cayman would grab it and drag it under.

Another threat came from deadly piranha fish. These fish have teeth like razors, and are attracted by blood.

They finished off the bits of flesh that the caymans left behind.

As the conquistadors crossed the river the Indians on the banks attacked. They were angry at these invaders who spoke a strange language and stole their canoes. They shot deadly, poisoned arrows at the soldiers. The soldiers fought back fiercely with their crossbows and powerful muskets.

Poisoned arrows

The forest echoed with the explosions of guns, the squeals of pigs and horses, and the cries of the wounded and dying. It was a terrifying time.

Musket

A musket is loaded with gunpowder, then a bullet. It fires when a flint creates a spark to explode the gunpowder and fire the bullet.

Finally the soldiers made it across the river. But their problems were far from over. Their way was now blocked by a deep gorge, where the river flowed between cliffs that were 1,200 feet (365 meters) high.

The conquistadors had to build a rope bridge. They managed to throw a rope across the gorge. A grappling hook on one end caught hold in the rocks on the far side. Then one brave man swung across and clambered up the opposite cliff. There he caught more ropes that were thrown to him, until enough stretched across the gap to build the bridge.

One by one the army crossed the gorge, trying not to look down at the river.

Eventually they reached another, wider river. They needed to build a boat so they could explore the riverbanks and look for food. But they were in a bad way. Most of the 4,000 Indians who started out with the soldiers had died. All of the pigs, dogs, and llamas had been eaten. More men died every day. Some of the soldiers were even tempted to become cannibals, and eat their comrades. They were so short of food that they began to chew their leather belts and their horses' saddles.

The conquistadors did not know how to hunt in the rainforest. The Indians who lived there hunted monkeys and tapirs by creeping up on them silently. When they were close enough they would shoot the animal with poisoned darts from their blowpipes.

When the conquistadors hunted they hacked their way through the trees. They made so much noise that they frightened the animals away.

Tapir
Tapirs are shy animals. They come down to rivers to eat water plants, but quickly vanish into the forest when people are around.

Night terrors

At night the soldiers huddled around a blazing camp fire.

The conquistadors were feared for their cruelty and violence, but now it was their turn to be frightened. In the shadows around them they imagined hordes of hostile Indians, waiting to pick them off one by one with poisoned darts. They sometimes thought they could see the glowing yellow eyes of man-eating jaguars.

They had also heard stories of the giant anaconda, a snake as long as five people laid end-to-end.

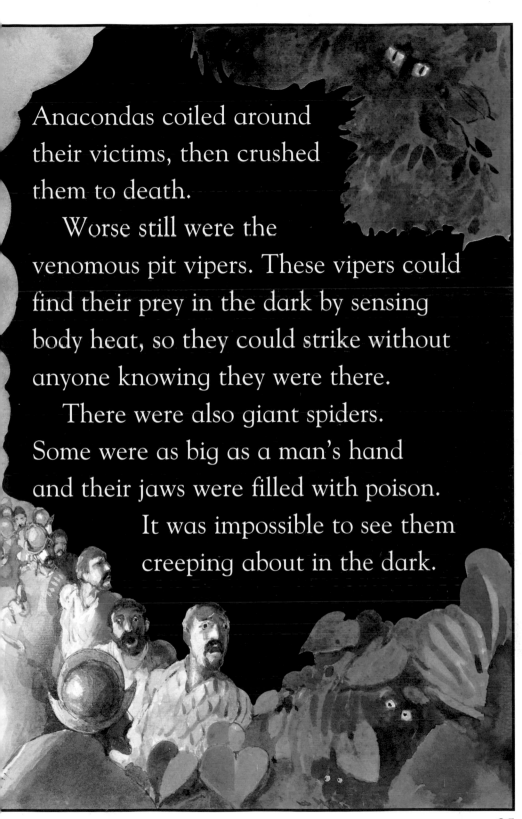

Anacondas coiled around
their victims, then crushed
them to death.

Worse still were the
venomous pit vipers. These vipers could
find their prey in the dark by sensing
body heat, so they could strike without
anyone knowing they were there.

There were also giant spiders.
Some were as big as a man's hand
and their jaws were filled with poison.
It was impossible to see them
creeping about in the dark.

Fireflies

Overhead, eerie pinpricks of light moved about. These were fireflies.

Night and day, the noises of the forest were deafening. Strange-looking birds let out calls that echoed through the forest. Thousands of crickets filled the air with their chirruping.

Toucans have huge colorful bills that are very light in weight.

Groups of howler monkeys in the treetops let out hideous screams. Tree frogs croaked all night.

Howler monkey

No one could sleep. Gonzalo Pizarro's soldiers were tired, starving and sick. They were covered with insect bites that itched, and they had had enough.

"We would rather die than go on," they told him. "Please do something to help us."

Poison dart frog

The bright colors of poison dart frogs warn other animals to leave them alone, because their skin contains a deadly poison.

Looking for help

Pizarro made one last desperate attempt to carry on. He ordered his most trusted captain, Francisco de Orellana, to build a boat and sail down river in search of food.

The conquistadors celebrated Christmas Day 1541 in the jungle, eating a Christmas dinner of roots and rats. Then Orellana set out with 57 soldiers. He promised to return in 12 days. The current carried their boat swiftly away.

Strangler fig

Strangler fig seeds germinate in the branches of rainforest trees. Their roots grow down the trunk. When the roots reach the soil, they swell, strangling the host tree.

The soldiers drifted downstream, between riverbanks where the forest reached right down to the water's edge. They passed palms, strangler figs, and towering rainforest trees covered in long vines called lianas, which dangled from the branches like ropes.

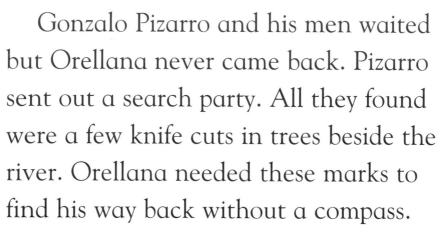

Gonzalo Pizarro and his men waited but Orellana never came back. Pizarro sent out a search party. All they found were a few knife cuts in trees beside the river. Orellana needed these marks to find his way back without a compass.

The soldiers could not tell whether Orellana and their comrades had deserted them, or had died. Perhaps their boat had been swept over a waterfall and they had drowned? When Orellana and his men vanished, the expedition's last hope of finding El Dorado disappeared with them.

Now Gonzalo Pizarro and the surviving conquistadors could only struggle back through the forest. They ate their last horse. They crossed back over the swaying rope bridge. Somehow they struggled back across the river, braving the caymans and the piranhas.

It took a long time to hack their way back through the forest that had grown up again behind them. But in August 1542, one and a half years after they set out, the weary survivors staggered into the town of Quito.

Less than half of the 210 soldiers who had set out on the search for El Dorado had returned. The ragged party carried nothing but their swords.

Where were they?

What happened to Francisco de Orellana, who had set out to find food? He hadn't deserted his comrades. His boat had been swept down river.

After eight days of drifting down river, Orellana's men heard drums in the forest. They found a village on the water's edge. Luckily, the Indians were friendly and gave the starving soldiers some food.

The soldiers were never sure which plants in the forest might be poisonous, and which ones they could eat. The Indians who lived there had learned which ones could be used for food. They grew a plant called cassava. Cassava is poisonous, but the Indians knew how to get rid of the poison.

Cassava root

Cassava leaves

First they ground the root up into a powder, then they washed away the poisons and roasted it into a kind of porridge. Their skill saved the lives of Orellana and his men.

Once Orellana and his men were strong enough, they drifted on downstream in their overcrowded boat. In the daytime they used large leaves to shade themselves from the heat of the sun. They had seen the Indians do this.

At night swarms of mosquitoes and biting flies made it impossible to sleep. Some soldiers caught a fever and died.

At times the river narrowed and they had to force their boat between giant, floating water lily leaves.

Each leaf was so big that a soldier could have laid across it with his arms stretched out and still not touched the edges.

When the river began to grow wider, the explorers realized that they would need a bigger boat. They made camp, cut down some trees, and built a stronger vessel.

Annatto

Annatto is a red dye made from the seeds of a small tree called Bixa orellana. The tree is named after Francisco de Orellana.

They met more Indian tribes as they drifted on down river. They saw tribes who dyed their skin scarlet with the juice of the annatto tree.

The strangest Indians in the Amazon were the "Cat People." They pushed long plant spines through their noses to look like cats' whiskers.

Jaguar

They wanted to look like jaguars because they believed these fierce cats were their ancestors.

Plant spines

Some rainforest tribes today still pierce their faces.

They reach the sea

Every day the banks of the river became more distant. Sometimes brightly colored flocks of macaws flew across the water. Often the mangrove trees along the riverbanks were covered in

Scarlet ibis

flocks of scarlet ibises.

Soon the soldiers could no longer see land. Had they reached the sea? It was hard to tell. But at last, in August 1542, when they tried to drink the water they found that it was salty.

Macaw

The soldiers had reached the Atlantic Ocean at the same time as Gonzalo Pizarro and his comrades struggled back into the town of Quito.

Of Captain Orellana's band of 57 soldiers, only 46 were still alive when they reached the sea.

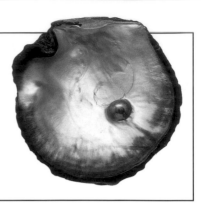

Pearls

Pearls grow inside oyster shells when a grain of sand gets stuck in the soft flesh of the animal inside. The sand is covered with layers of pearl.

Orellana and his men sailed along the coast until they reached an island. There they found a village of pearl fishermen who gave them food and shelter. They welcomed the rest.

Then the soldiers set sail for Spain, 4,000 miles (6,436 km) away on the other side of the Atlantic Ocean.

When they finally reached home they told fantastic stories of their ordeal. Stories of giant snakes, man-eating fish, and Indian tribes whose poisoned darts brought a slow, agonizing death. Tales of terrifying nights in the forest and days spent struggling for survival.

The strangest story of all told of a tribe of giant women warriors who had attacked Orellana and his soldiers.

The ancient Greeks passed down stories about these mythical warriors who were experts at fighting with the bow and arrow. They were known as Amazons. Even the ancient Greeks had believed that Amazons had died out, but now Orellana claimed to have found them. Orellana could not have seen them. They do not exist. Perhaps the terrible heat, sickness, and fear made the men believe that they had.

But the conquistadors claimed that they had found the land of the Amazons during their adventure. And that is how the Amazon forest and the Amazon River got their names.

The conquistadors' biggest disappointment was their failure to find El Dorado.

Francisco de Orellana went back again to look for El Dorado in 1545, but he died on the voyage. No one has ever found the golden city.

But some people
still believe it is to be found in the
Amazon rainforest – somewhere hidden
among the trees...

Glossary

Ambitious
People who are ambitious hope that they will get everything that they want.

Ancestor
A person who lived in the past, and who is a distant relative of people who are alive today.

Andes
A long line of high mountains that stretch all the way down the west side of South America.

Atlantic
The ocean which lies between Europe and America.

Conquistadors
Spanish noblemen who set out to explore and conquer South America in search of treasure. They were fierce and cruel fighters.

Creek
A small stream that flows into a river.

Fireflies
Insects that produce flashes of light. This makes them easy to see at night.

Gorge
A steep-sided valley, where rocks have been worn away by a fast-flowing river.

Grappling hook
A hook with three or four points that is tied to the end of a rope. The hook can be thrown and used to grip things that are out of reach.

Legend
A story from history that has been told over and over again, but which has not been proved to be true.

Lianas
Climbing plants that grow up into the branches of trees, then dangle down like ropes.

Machete
A large knife with a heavy, flat blade. It is ideal for cutting tough plant stems.

Malaria
A dangerous disease caused when people are bitten by mosquitoes. As the animal sucks blood it injects the disease into its victim.

Mangrove
A type of plant that grows in the mud along the banks of tropical rivers.

Myth
A well-known story that is not really true. It is often about imaginary people.

Rainforest
A tropical forest where the air is always warm and wet.

Spices
These are dried parts of plants that can be used to make food tastier, or used to make things smell good.

Tribe
A group of people who worship the same gods and who all share the same way of living.